S0-AJP-254

21st Century Disasters

East African Drought of 2011

by Sue Gagliardi

FOCUS READERS

BEACON

www.focusreaders.com

Copyright © 2020 by Focus Readers, Lake Elmo, MN 55042. All rights reserved. No part of this book may be reproduced or utilized in any form or by any means without written permission from the publisher.

Focus Readers is distributed by North Star Editions:
sales@northstareditions.com | 888-417-0195

Produced for Focus Readers by Red Line Editorial.

Photographs ©: Rebecca Blackwell/AP Images, cover, 1, 4; Retta Lemma/Oxfam/AP Images, 7; Naruedom Yaempongsa/Shutterstock Images, 8; Melih Cevdet Teksen/Shutterstock Images, 10, 29; guenterguni/iStockphoto, 13; Red Line Editorial, 14; SimplyCreativePhotography/iStockphoto, 16–17; EcoPrint/Shutterstock Images, 18; sirichai chinprayoon/Shutterstock Images, 21; mustafa olgun/Shutterstock Images, 23; sadikgulec/iStockphoto, 24; journalturk/iStockphoto, 26

Library of Congress Cataloging-in-Publication Data
Names: Gagliardi, Sue, 1969- author.
Title: East African drought of 2011 / by Sue Gagliardi.
Description: Lake Elmo, MN : Focus Readers, [2020] | Series: 21st century
  disasters | Audience: Grades 4 to 6. | Includes bibliographical references
  and index.
Identifiers: LCCN 2019002422 (print) | LCCN 2019004766 (ebook) | ISBN
  9781641859448 (pdf) | ISBN 9781641858755 (ebook) | ISBN 9781641857376
  (hardcover) | ISBN 9781641858069 (pbk.)
Subjects: LCSH: Droughts--Africa, East--21st century--Juvenile literature. |
  Famines--Africa, East--21st century--Juvenile literature. | Africa,
  East--21st century--Juvenile literature.
Classification: LCC QC929.28.A353 (ebook) | LCC QC929.28.A353 G34 2020
  (print) | DDC 363.34/929--dc23
LC record available at https://lccn.loc.gov/2019002422

Printed in the United States of America
Mankato, MN
May, 2019

About the Author

Sue Gagliardi writes fiction, nonfiction, and poetry for children. Her books include *Fairies, Get Outside in Winter,* and *Get Outside in Spring.* Her work appears in children's magazines including *Highlights Hello, Highlights High Five, Ladybug,* and *Spider.* She teaches kindergarten and lives in Pennsylvania with her husband and son.

Chapter 1

Months Without Rain

Ten-year-old Hindiya gathered her goats. Her family lived in Kenya. To earn money, Hindiya's parents sold animals. The animals needed food. But it hadn't rained in months. The ground was dry. Crops withered.

Many people in East Africa raise goats and camels to earn money.

People ran out of food and water. Some families had to leave their homes. They walked for days in search of water. Hindiya and her family traveled for 17 days. They camped wherever they found water. They stayed until the water was gone. Then they moved on.

Hindiya and her family grew tired and hungry. But they kept going. They were dealing with a severe drought. A drought is a long period with little or no rain. In 2011, a

 When drought hits an area, people and animals struggle to find enough water.

drought affected millions of people.
It spread throughout the Horn
of Africa.

The Horn of Africa is located on the continent's eastern side.

The Horn of Africa is a **peninsula** in East Africa. It includes Kenya, Ethiopia, Somalia, and other nearby countries. Many people in this area are farmers. They depend on rain to grow their crops. But in 2010, very little rain fell. Less rain meant many people would have no food. By 2011, **famine** spread across the region.

Did You Know?

In East Africa, people plant small gardens called shambas. They grow vegetables and fruit trees to feed their families.

Chapter 2

Understanding Droughts

A drought happens when an area gets less rain than usual. The Horn of Africa typically has two rainy seasons each year. The long rains come in March through June. They bring most of the annual rainfall.

Children in Ethiopia carry water during a drought in 2016.

That is the total amount of rain a region gets all year. The short rains fall from October to December. They bring less rain than the long rains. But they are still important.

People depend on these rainy seasons. Many East Africans raise animals and crops. Without enough rain, the ground dries up. Plants cannot grow. People and animals run out of food.

From March to June of 2010, much less rain fell than usual.

 Drought can cause water holes to dry up.

The short rains that year were also below average. Within a few weeks, drought gripped the region.

DROUGHT TIMELINE

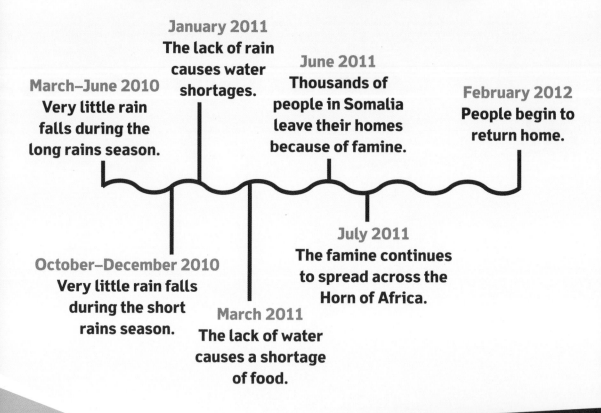

March–June 2010
Very little rain falls during the long rains season.

January 2011
The lack of rain causes water shortages.

June 2011
Thousands of people in Somalia leave their homes because of famine.

February 2012
People begin to return home.

October–December 2010
Very little rain falls during the short rains season.

March 2011
The lack of water causes a shortage of food.

July 2011
The famine continues to spread across the Horn of Africa.

Crops died. Grass for animals to eat dried up as well.

Many things can affect a region's rainfall. Weather patterns such as La Niña often play a role. La Niña cools the water of the Pacific Ocean. It also causes strong winds to blow. These winds pull moisture away from East Africa. As a result, East Africa receives less rain than usual. A strong La Niña in 2010 helped caused the 2011 drought.

Did You Know?

El Niño is another weather pattern. It warms the water of the Pacific Ocean.

Droughts

During a drought, people must **conserve** water. Farmers can choose **irrigation** systems that use less water. People can use barrels to collect any rain that does fall. They can drink the rainwater. Or they can use it to water crops.

Having enough food is also important. Before a drought, people stock up. They store food such as cereal and grain. They can eat this food during the drought. People can also plant crops that grow well in dry soil. These crops can survive with less water. People can eat or sell the crops during the drought.

Building a dam can help people store rainwater.

Chapter 3

Survivor Stories

A drought makes the ground very dry. Many plants die. Food and water become scarce. Farmers struggle to grow enough to eat or sell. For example, Dama Katana Ngonbo had a farm in Kenya.

 Dust blows across dry ground in Kenya during a drought.

The drought killed all of Dama's crops. She needed more water. So, Dama and her neighbors dug a well.

The well reached water deep underground. Dama used a bucket on a string to draw water from the well. Then she carried the water to her fields. There, she poured it over her crops.

Did You Know?

The 2011 drought was the worst drought to hit East Africa in 60 years.

 In drip irrigation, tubes release water near the roots of plants.

Some farmers used drip irrigation. In this system, water drips slowly onto the roots of plants. Very little water **evaporates**. This method helps farmers use less water.

Even so, many people ran out of water. Many were forced to leave their homes. Some families had to split up. Zeynab Hassan's husband went to search for water. Zeynab stayed with their five children. She gathered and sold wood. She used the money to buy food and water.

Did You Know?

During each month of 2011, approximately 15,000 people left Somalia. They traveled to nearby countries to escape the drought.

 Girls in Somalia often have to carry water long distances during droughts.

Getting enough wood was hard work. Zeynab often walked 20 miles (32 km) each day. She and her children survived. But she didn't know when she would see her husband again.

Chapter 4

After the Drought

The drought created a **crisis**. More than 13 million people were in need of help. People became sick or weak from lack of food and water. Some even died. And many others had to leave their homes.

 A woman gets water from a well at a refugee camp.

 Families stand outside their temporary shelters in the Dadaab camps in Kenya.

Thousands of people fled to **refugee camps**. The camps had food and clean water. They also provided medical care. Huge numbers of people lived together in the camps. Some camps became too full.

Scientists work to **predict** droughts. They track how much rain falls. They also look for weather patterns such as La Niña. They warn people if a drought is likely. They also guess how bad the drought might be. That way, people have more time to prepare.

Did You Know?

In August 2011, more than 400,000 people lived in the Dadaab camps near the border of Kenya and Somalia.

East African Drought of 2011

Write your answers on a separate piece of paper.

1. Write a sentence summarizing the main idea of Chapter 2.

2. If a drought affected your home, would you leave or stay? Why?

3. What is the name for the total amount of rain an area gets in one year?
   - **A.** severe drought
   - **B.** annual rainfall
   - **C.** irrigation system

4. Why does La Niña help cause droughts?
   - **A.** It causes winds that pull moisture away.
   - **B.** It causes animals to drink more water than usual.
   - **C.** It causes scientists to have trouble predicting the weather.

5. What does **withered** mean in this book?

*The ground was dry. Crops **withered**.*

    A. grew faster because of bright sun
    B. blew away in strong wind
    C. dried up from lack of water

6. What does **scarce** mean in this book?

*Many plants die. Food and water become **scarce**. Farmers struggle to grow enough to eat or sell.*

    A. very hard to find
    B. very easy to grow
    C. very big and heavy

Answer key on page 32.

Glossary

conserve
To prevent something from being used up or wasted.

crisis
A time of great danger or serious problems.

evaporates
Changes from liquid to gas.

famine
An extreme shortage of food.

irrigation
The process of watering crops though human-made means, such as pipes.

peninsula
An area of land surrounded on three sides by water.

predict
To guess or estimate what might happen in the future.

refugee camps
Places where people can live when they are forced to leave their homes due to war or other dangers.

To Learn More

BOOKS

Chambers, Catherine. *Can We Protect People from Natural Disasters?* Chicago: Heinemann Raintree, 2015.

Meister, Cari. *Droughts*. Minneapolis: Pogo Books, 2016.

Merrick, Patrick. *Droughts*. Mankato, MN: The Child's World, 2015.

NOTE TO EDUCATORS

Visit **www.focusreaders.com** to find lesson plans, activities, links, and other resources related to this title.

Index

Answer Key: 1. Answers will vary; 2. Answers will vary; 3. B; 4. A; 5. C; 6. A